MW00813537

I Chose You

I Chose You

Written *by* LINDSEY SHUMWAY
Illustrated by AMY HINTZE

© 2005 Text Lindsey Shumway
© 2005 Illustrations Amy Hintze

All rights reserved.

No part of this book may be reproduced in any form whatsoever, whether by graphic, visual, electronic, film, microfilm, tape recording, or any other means, without prior written permission of the author and illustrator, except in the case of brief passages embodied in critical reviews and articles.

ISBN: 1-55517-861-8
v.1

Published by CFI,
an imprint of Cedar Fort, Inc.
925 N. Main Springville, Utah, 84663
www.cedarfort.com

Distributed by:

Cover and book design by Nicole Williams
Cover design © 2005 by Lyle Mortimer

Printed in Hong Kong
10 9 8 7 6 5 4 3 2 1

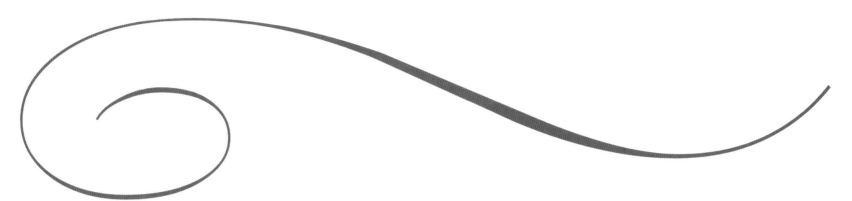

AUTHOR'S DEDICATION

For my mother, who told me this story as many times as I
needed to hear it. Also to the precious angels I chose—
I love you more than you will ever know.

ARTIST'S DEDICATION

To my loving husband, Brian—without him,
this never could have happened.

One day in heaven a long time ago, Heavenly Father led me by the hand into a big room filled with children.

He told me that today was a special day; it was the day I got to pick out my very own child.

There was a long, long line of boys and girls. They were all different and special in their own way.

Some were short,

and others were tall.

Some had curly hair, and some had straight hair.

Some liked playing soccer,

and others liked playing with animals.

Some were really good at math,

and others were good at painting.

Some of the girls
liked dresses,
and others liked jeans.

Some of the boys liked baseball,

and others liked swimming.

Some were especially kind to others,

and some were good at making people laugh.

Some loved football,

and others loved camping.

Some were really good at spelling,

and others were good at drawing.

Some liked computers, and others loved video games.

Some liked dancing,

and others liked singing.

Some were good at sharing,

and some were good at
picking up their rooms.

Some liked making sand castles,

and others liked making mud pies.

Each one was so different and beautiful that I
had to walk up and down that line for a long time.

I looked at every one of those children.

And I chose you.